An Amish Spring Rose

By
Ruth Bawell

Table of Contents

Unsolicited Testimonials

By **Phyllis**

⭐⭐⭐⭐⭐ Love Ruth!

I love Ruth's books! Her mysteries are the best!

⭐⭐⭐⭐⭐ Love This Author

Ruth Bawell is very creative and a great writer! All her books have left me unable to stop reading till the ending! There were a few Amish fact mistakes, like unmarried man having a beard, but the plot was so good I overlooked that!

By **Steve M**

⭐⭐⭐⭐⭐ I love romance stories August 5, 2017

I love romance stories... well written with her usual twists to the story still enjoyed them very much Once I start I can't put it down.

By **Bones**

⭐⭐⭐⭐⭐ Amish County Stories

I love all the Amish County stories! Each one brings so much excitement! Ruth Bawell is also a wonderful writer!

By **Kindle Customer**

⭐⭐⭐⭐⭐ Good clean writing.

The Amish stories of Ruth Bawell are authentic, faith-filled writings. They are short, more the length of novellas or longer short stories. Always clean, always uplifting.

CHAPTER ONE

"*Guder Nummidaag.*" A pleasant baritone drew Rose out of her reverie by the window, and she turned around to see a young man standing right behind her.

"Oh!" she exclaimed, stepping back almost guiltily and smoothing down her apron. "*Guder Nummidaag* to you too! And welcome to Honeycrest Inn!"

She looked up into a pair of dark, brooding eyes under a straw hat and blinked uncertainly.

"I'm sorry, may I help you?" she asked, realizing from his attire that he belonged to their community, though she didn't recall seeing him around in their village.

The young man doffed his hat, revealing a thick mop of dark hair, and gave her a bright smile. "I'm aware I'm late for your lunch service, but my clients, whom I am to meet here, have expressed their desire to have a meal at your lovely Inn, and I couldn't disappoint them… Though I am aware that this is very short notice and you probably don't have any Shoofly Pie left over."

Rose gave the young man a reassuring smile. "Please don't worry. We haven't run out of anything, and even if we had, we would do everything in our power to serve you just the meal you desire." She was momentarily thrown off guard because the dark-haired stranger was studying her face as if he was searching for an answer to something. "My name is Rose, by the way. Rose Stoltzfus."

"Rose," he said, his voice just above a whisper, "pleased to meet you." His eyes pinned hers down. "I'm Jason Lehman."

"Oh," Rose replied. "Are you from Lehman's Farm?"

"I am," Jason nodded.

"Please, do be seated," Rose said, guiding Jason to a table and looking around for a waiter. Realizing that most of the staff would have gone off duty, she promptly went to work herself and began to take Jason's order.

"Have you worked here long?" Jason asked, picking up the menu and running his eyes over it.

Rose gave him a self-deprecatory smile. "My family owns the Inn, and I run this restaurant," she replied. She didn't add that she was only twenty years old, and that it was quite an achievement for one so young to run a restaurant so successfully such as theirs.

"Oh! That's wonderful," Jason remarked.

"I'm the chef," Rose added.

"Even better," Jason said, "because you can then advise me on what I should order before my guests arrive." He grinned. "We need to give the Englischers the finest Amish cuisine they've ever had."

"Of course," Rose agreed, nodding rapidly, though she felt a surge of apprehension. It was going to be difficult waitressing while also getting the meal ready.

"Again, I'm sorry for coming in so late, when your staff have obviously gone off for their own lunch break," Jason said.

"That's quite alright," Rose replied. Her bright smile hid any misgivings she might have as Jason rattled off his order.

***

"The finest meal we've had in a long while," one of Jason's guests said. "The Scrapple and Shoofly Pie were particularly delicious!"

"Thank you for serving us Scrapple, though it's not on your lunch menu," Jason chimed in.

"You're welcome," Rose replied politely, glad she had had some of their traditional breakfast food to serve Jason's guests.

"Frankly, I could eat Scrapple any time of day," Jason added. "I hope you have some should I show up unexpectedly again, Rose." He smiled kindly as he spoke, and his eyes shone when he looked at her.

The way he said her name caused an unfamiliar flutter in Rose's tummy. She swallowed. "Of course," she said. "You're welcome to come any time you like."

She hurriedly escaped to the kitchen, taking refuge amongst the pots and pans and the shiny work surfaces that she began to scrub down vigorously.

"Did those customers that you were waiting on give you a tough time?" Martha Stoltzfus, Rose's mother, asked. She had stopped by the kitchen after finishing her afternoon chores.

"On the contrary, *Mamm*," Rose replied, "they were very appreciative."

"Well, they should be," Martha retorted. "It's way past lunch service, and they obviously made some difficult requests, judging by your expression. How did you manage without the waiting staff?"

"I was fine, *Mamm*," Rose answered. "And I am still fine." She wrinkled her nose. "What do you mean, my expression?" she queried.

"You seem flustered," Martha observed, eyeing her daughter keenly.

Rose flushed. She was flustered, but not for the reasons her mother imagined.

"I'm alright, *Mamm*," Rose said. "But perhaps we should have a couple of waiters available through the day, just in case customers come in for a late lunch or an early tea."

"I agree," Martha said, nodding. "We can ask to take their lunch break at different times." She shook her head. "Why didn't we think of that before?"

"I suppose spring just crept up on us," Rose answered with a grin. "The tourist traffic into the village has increased, and I guess we just didn't plan for the lunch rush to come."

Martha sighed. "You're right. The rooms are full too, unlike in winter."

"Is Luke alright?" Rose asked. "I haven't seen him all day, and I just hope he hasn't missed me too much."

"He was with me for a while and is now with your *daed*," her mother replied.

"I hope the spring rush isn't going to be too hard on Luke," Rose said anxiously. "He's still so young."

"He will get used to things," Martha replied. "Like he has already. The Lord has been good and given Luke the ability to adapt."

Rose nodded. "He has indeed," she said, her mind going back to a day three years ago, as ordinary as any other day, when their lives were turned upside down.

"He had been through some hard times. We all have," Martha remarked, reading her daughter's thoughts.

Rose nodded, biting her lip. It had been devastating, to say the least. She remembered being told that her sister Grace and brother-in-law Reuben were no more. They had lost their lives in a buggy accident, leaving behind their son Luke, not even a year old at the time.

"The only reason that little Luke didn't suffer any greater trauma was because of you, Rose," Martha said. "You have been a mother to him."

"I love him so much," Rose said, thinking of her sister with a sad smile.

After her mother had gone, Rose flopped down on a chair in the restaurant. She had never felt quite so strange before—disturbed and exhilarated all at once. Disturbed, because she always felt that way when she thought back to the day her sister and brother-in-law had died… and exhilarated because of the appreciation she had just received. She gazed across at the table where only minutes before, a group of guests had sat enjoying a meal she had prepared and served with care.

Rose placed her hands on her belly. She couldn't stop the flutter there, and neither could she seem to blank out the image of Jason's dark, haunting eyes as they lingered on hers.

"You're being silly, Rose," she said to herself. *"Jason's eyes didn't linger on yours. You're being fanciful."*

Her inner dialogue continued, *"But they seemed to look right into you."*

She stood up and paced about the empty restaurant. *"No,"* she said to herself. *"He was just being pleasant, as any customer would who wanted the best service for their guests. Particularly if they were going to be discussing business over the meal."*

Rose took a deep breath. *"Yes,"* she told herself, *"Jason was merely being nice, so that the meal impressed his guests, and led to them making a good business deal."*

Having come to that conclusion, Rose felt immensely better and in control of her emotions once again. And after she had eaten some food herself, the flutter in her tummy disappeared, and she concluded that she had probably just been hungry all along.

CHAPTER TWO

Riding home in his buggy, Jason Lehman found his thoughts dwelling on the young girl at Honeycrest Inn. Rose seemed an apt name for one of such rare charm. He would have to see her again, to be sure. And her Scrapple was the best he had ever eaten, though he hadn't told her that for fear of seeming disloyal to his *mamm*—her recipe for Scrapple was the most sought after in the Lehman family.

He would definitely have to visit Honeycrest Inn again. Just for the food, of course, and also for the ambiance which had so lifted his spirits and those of his guests, who had expressed a desire to meet there again.

Jason took a deep breath of the fresh spring air. He felt elated. His business deal had gone through, and at just twenty-four years old, he was the only Stud Farm owner in Pinewood Village. Jacob Lehman, Jason's father, had had his doubts when his son decided to go exclusively into stud farming rather than join the family livestock trade, but he had encouraged him and was proud of his accomplishments. Jason wore his success well and was not in any way changed by it. He remained humble, and if anything, he worked harder.

"Jason," his mother, Lydia, greeted him as he entered their home. "You've been gone all day, son. Have you even eaten since breakfast?"

"I had to entertain some clients, *Mamm*," Jason explained as he shrugged off his coat and rolled up his sleeves. "And yes, I did eat—at Honeycrest Inn."

"Oh! I have been hearing a lot about the place," Lydia remarked. "Martha and John Stoltzfus run the Inn, and their daughter Rose takes care of the restaurant. I heard, though so very young—just twenty years old—Rose is a fine cook and does our Amish cuisine proud."

Jason felt a strange, yet not unpleasant, sensation somewhere in the region of his chest.

"So, how was the food, son?" Lydia queried.

"It was very good," Jason replied. "Rose…" His voice trailed off and he felt his throat constrict. He had never felt anything like this before.

"Rose…?" Lydia prompted.

Jason swallowed and cleared his throat. "She is a very good chef," he managed to say, realizing that it was difficult to say Rose's name without feeling like he couldn't breathe.

"You must take me there to sample the food," Lydia said. "But you seem flushed. Are you alright?"

"Yes," Jason replied, flexing his suspenders. They felt suddenly tighter across his rib cage. "I finalized a very good deal with my clients, and they will pick up the horses next week."

"Well done, son," Lydia smiled.

"I will see you in a little while, *Mamm*," Jason said. "I have to check on the horses, and *Daed* wanted some help with a cow who's about to give birth."

Jason hurried away before his mother could detain him further. As he strode rapidly towards the byre, he tried to say Rose's name, but once again found that he couldn't get it past his throat. This was a new experience, and disconcerting, because Jason began to wonder how he would address Rose if he couldn't even say her name out loud.

"Jason, my boy," Jacob greeted his son as he walked into the barn. "You're just in time to help with this latest birth."

Jason rolled his sleeves up further as he approached and hunkered down by his father, next to the cow. "I'd have missed it if I had taken any longer," he replied.

"Where have you been all day?" Jacob asked, his eyes on the animal before them.

"Sealing a large business deal," Jason answered, "over a delicious, authentic Amish meal."

"Ah," Jacob remarked. "Was it at Honeycrest Inn?"

"How did you guess?" Jason queried, surprised.

"Well, everybody's been talking about the place and the food. The Inn is very popular with the Englischers, and the restaurant there is…" Jacob paused mid-sentence to more closely observe the cow.

"Divine," Jason murmured.

"What was that?" Jacob asked.

"The calf's going to drop any minute now," Jason replied, trying to change the subject.

His father looked at him out of the corner of his eye. "I heard you say Divine. You aren't planning to name the calf that, are you?" Jacob laughed.

"No, *Daed*," Jason answered with an awkward chuckle. "I was completing your sentence, saying the restaurant at Honeycrest Inn is divine."

Their conversation was interrupted as the young calf made its way into the world. "There it comes," Jacob said, and he and Jason let out a whoop of joy together.

"No matter how many of these births I see, it always seems like the first time, doesn't it, *Daed*?" Jason remarked.

"It sure does, son," Jacob replied. "But you know what I'm really waiting for?"

"What?" Jason queried.

"For the birth of your first baby, and your second, and, well, your third and fourth," Jacob replied.

"*Daed*," Jason answered, inexplicably flustered. "I'm not even close to courtship, and you're thinking of my children?"

"Well, which parent doesn't dream of becoming a grandparent?" Jacob countered.

"Dream away, *Daed*," Jason laughed, as they left the byre.

"I'm allowed to, aren't I?" Jacob replied with a smile. He patted his son on the back. "So, you sealed a big deal then, did you?" he asked.

Jason nodded. "I did, *Daed*," he answered.

"And I'm so proud of you," Jacob said. "But there's one big deal that I hope you'll seal soon."

"And which one is that?" Jason asked.

"Asking a nice young girl to marry you," Jacob replied.

"But *Daed*…" Jason began to protest.

"Surely there are some nice young girls that you have been meeting from time to time…and perhaps the thought of courting one of them has crossed your mind," Jacob said.

"Not really," Jason replied. "Because I hadn't ever met someone that I wanted to get to know better, or court… or marry."

"Oh, you *hadn't met*? Does that mean you've met someone now?" Jacob asked with a chuckle.

"No, oh no," Jason said hurriedly. "I meant I haven't met anybody, *Daed*."

"Well, when the time is right, son, the right girl will come along and leave you breathless," Jacob declared.

"Breathless?" Jason queried, remembering his difficulty catching his breath around Rose. "How so?"

"I'm just being unusually poetic for a cattle farmer," Jacob laughed. "But I remember how I always felt like I couldn't breathe when I was in the vicinity of the girl I married."

"*Mamm*? She made you feel like you couldn't breathe?" Jason asked, amused.

"Oh yes, son," Jacob replied. "What's more, I felt tongue-tied around her. I probably almost gave myself a heart attack when the time came to ask if I could court her."

Jason heaved a silent sigh of relief. He hadn't been in the least tongue-tied around any woman, even Rose. As for the whole thing about not being able to breathe… of course he could. He was just being absurd.

***

At the Stoltzfus home, Rose sat down to supper with Martha and John Stoltzfus, her nephew Luke, and her brothers Matthew and Silas.

"I'm so glad we live right next door to the Inn," Rose remarked, picking Luke up and setting him down on her lap.

"Yes, it's so convenient," Martha said, nodding.

From where she was seated at the table, Rose could look out of the window at the Inn. It looked quaint and mysterious in the twilight with the lamplit windows aglow. The sound of birds going home to roost filled the air, and Rose felt a warm cloud of tranquility settle around her shoulders like a shawl.

"I liked the stew, *Mamm*," Luke said, as Rose wiped his mouth with the edge of her apron.

"I'm so glad you did, my little baby," Rose cooed. Nobody had the heart to dissuade Luke from thinking of Rose as his mother after he had lost his own when he was just an infant. But Rose was aware that sooner or later, Luke would be asking why he didn't have a *daed* like all the other children, and she didn't quite know how she would respond to the question.

"You look like you need an early night," Martha remarked.

"Yes," Rose replied with a yawn. "And I have an early start tomorrow."

"Yes, you do," Martha said. "You need to prepare and pack a picnic lunch for the guests going out for the day with your *daed*."

"*Daed*," Rose said, turning to her father. "Would you be able to take Luke with you on the picnic? That way, I can get ahead on a batch of pies."

"Of course," John replied.

"Picnic," Luke repeated.

"Yes, my beautiful boy," Rose cooed, "Would you like to go with *Groosdaadi* for a picnic?"

Luke nodded, slid off Rose's lap, and climbed onto John's knee.

"Rose, you go to bed, child. I'll get Luke washed and ready for bed," Martha said, as Rose yawned again.

"Thank you, *Mamm*," Rose replied gratefully.

CHAPTER THREE

Rose weighed out the flour and butter for a batch of pies and began to work the butter into the flour with her fingertips. As she worked, her thoughts went to Luke and the way he had become a part of her life. In fact, she couldn't think of her life without him in it. He was not only a reminder of her sister Grace, but from the first moment that she'd held him after she had heard that Grace and Reuben were no more, she'd felt like Luke was her responsibility… like Grace was pleading with her not to leave her little boy alone.

"It's best for Luke to be attached to you, Rose," Martha had said through her tears. "Because you are young and can be there for him for longer than we can."

"*Mamm*, don't say that," Rose had protested, but she knew that her mother was right. Luke needed a mother as much as he needed his grandparents and his uncles Matthew and Silas. So the Stoltzfus family had come together and helped Luke through the tragedy, even as they helped each other through the pain of losing Grace and Reuben so suddenly.

"*Mamm*," Martha would say, holding Luke and pointing to Rose. "Say *mamm*, Luke, my boy."

Rose felt her heart swell as it always did when she recalled the first time Luke had called her *Mamm*. She had held him tight and kissed his beautiful pink hands and loved him even more as if he were her own.

"If anything were ever to happen to me," Grace had once said to her, *"You'll be there for Lukey and any other children I might have, won't you, Rosie?"*

"Well, nothing's going to happen to you, sis," Rose had replied. *"But I will be there for your children. I already am. I can't wait for Luke to call me Ant Rose!"*

But as fate would have it, Luke never called Rose *Ant*, and never would. And she would keep her promise to Grace and be there for him. She wouldn't ever let Grace down, or Luke. She was his *mamm*, no matter what.

"There's a customer asking to speak to you," Annie, one of the serving staff, announced.

Rose was so deep in her thoughts that she didn't hear Annie the first time, and jumped when Annie finally came up and tapped her on the shoulder.

"What's wrong?" Rose asked.

"There's a customer who wishes to speak with you, Rose," Annie replied.

Rose hastily wiped her hands on her apron, then threw it off and put on a fresh one. Adjusting her *kaap*, she went out to see who the customer was, hoping it wasn't about a complaint.

"Jason!" Rose exclaimed in surprise. It had been a few weeks since his first visit, and she had wondered if she would ever see him again.

Jason surveyed her in silence for what seemed like a very long while. The seconds stretched out. Rose didn't know that he was struggling to say her name.

"How are you?" Jason said eventually, feeling a flush rise to his cheeks.

"I'm well, thank you," Rose replied. "Are my staff looking after you?"

"I just came in, actually," Jason said. "I'm here to meet some new clients and treat them to some of your exquisite food."

"Well, as it happens, I have some Scrapple ready and waiting, even though it's past breakfast time," Rose declared with a smile.

"I made it a point to come in early for lunch," Jason said, his eyes on hers as if he was searching them for something.

"You're well in time to beat rush hour," Rose replied. "What do you have in mind for your meal today?" Noticing that Jason was still standing, Rose added, "And please do be seated."

"Perhaps you'd help me choose something for us?" Jason said. He was struggling to keep his voice even.

"I'd be happy to," Rose answered. "We have our signature roast on the menu. I can guarantee that no *Englischer* would have ever had a traditional Amish roast, with spring vegetables on the side and, of course, Scrapple. I also highly recommend our cabbage rolls and apple dumplings."

She paused, breathless, waiting for a reaction, but Jason had his eyes fixed on hers and appeared to be in some kind of reverie.

"As I was saying," Rose continued, "the cabbage rolls…"

"I say yes to it all… and anything else you recommend," Jason declared, his deep baritone now a resonant whisper. He paused in the manner of one who takes a bite out of a delicious morsel of food and savors it, and then spoke her name. "Rose."

When he said her name, Rose felt the strange flutter in her tummy that she had experienced when she first met him. This was odd, she thought to herself. She hadn't felt it since, and now… now it almost choked her up.

She nodded rapidly. "How soon… umm…will your guests… take to get here?" she managed to say, stammering through the question.

"They'll be here soon," Jason replied. "But don't let that worry you. Though if you could lay on something to nibble on while we wait for the meal, that would be nice."

"I'll get you some appetizers," Rose said, trying to keep her voice even, and hurried away.

"Is that him?" Martha queried, coming into the kitchen.

"Who?" Rose asked, turning to her mother.

"Jason Lehman. The most successful twenty-four-year-old in the village," Martha answered with a grin.

"Yes," Rose replied.

"Is that his order?" Martha asked, scanning the order slip that Rose had pinned up.

"Yes," Rose answered again.

"No wonder you look flushed," Martha observed. "That's a lot of food to prepare. How many people is he expecting?"

Rose shrugged and wordlessly got started on getting the appetizers out.

"He must really love your food," Martha remarked, scanning the order slip again. "Or else…" Her voice trailed off as she gave her daughter a searching look.

"What's wrong, *Mamm*?" Rose asked anxiously. "Have we run out of something?"

Martha shook her head and gave Rose another long look. "I'll help you," she said.

"You will?" Rose asked.

"Yes. You need help and I'm here," Martha declared, throwing on an apron and getting to work. "All our guests have gone on the picnic with your *daed*, so I've nothing else to do."

"I hope Luke is enjoying the picnic," Rose remarked.

"So, what's he like?" Martha asked, not letting Ruth change the subject.

"Who?" Rose queried, arranging buttermilk biscuits topped with ham and cheese on a platter.

"Jason Lehman," Martha replied. "And I do like your new creation. Those bite-sized biscuits make a delicious appetizer."

"I have just met him twice," Rose said, "so I really don't know what Jason Lehman is truly like, though he seems like a good person." So saying, she swept past the serving staff and carried the trays out herself.

Jason stood up when Rose approached, balancing two trays of appetizers on her palms, and did the unthinkable. He met her halfway across the floor and took the trays from her. As she began to protest, Jason gave her a reassuring smile.

"It's alright, Rose," he said. "Please don't treat me like a guest."

Rose looked up into his eyes and nodded, wondering if she was dreaming. She then became aware that his guests had arrived, so she gave them a bright smile and proceeded to introduce the dish, even as she gave them a detailed description of the meal to come.

"And I'd better return to preparing it, or it might just remain something that you heard about but never tasted," Rose finished. Turning around, she walked briskly back to the kitchen.

"What a silly remark," she said aloud as she entered the kitchen. Her mother looked enquiringly at her.

"What? Jason Lehman made a silly remark? At you?" Martha asked, aghast.

"No, *Mamm*!" Rose answered. *"I* made a silly remark about the food remaining something that the guests would have heard about but never tasted, if I didn't hurry back here and prepare it."

"Actually, that's a clever remark, Rose," Martha said, beaming. "Who knew our Rose was both witty as well as a brilliant cook!"

Inwardly, she was also smiling. If Rose was that worried about her remarks, she must like this boy very much indeed.

***

"We loved the food!" one of Jason's guests said, as Rose went out to see how their meal was progressing.

"And I sure am glad it was something we got to taste, and feast on, rather than only hear about," one of the others declared with a laugh.

Rose laughed with them, but as her gaze drifted from the guests to Jason, something in his eyes made her hold her breath. The flutter in her tummy felt like an army of butterflies now.

"Oh, dear," she murmured, "I need to get back to the kitchen. There are more orders to take care of."

***

As Jason drove away, he felt like he had left something behind at the restaurant in Honeycrest

Inn. He wished he had thanked Rose personally, but she had rushed away and not returned. She seemed flustered, but that was only natural when the restaurant was so full. He would need to go across and thank her personally soon.

He smiled to himself. At least he had managed to say her name. But her eyes—he still couldn't figure them out. Were they golden, hazel or amber? How very beautiful they were, and so expressive. And that moment, when they had alighted on his, he had been spellbound, speechless, tongue-tied. And then she had rushed away before he had had the chance to recover his powers of speech and tell her how grateful he was for extending herself yet again—so much so that he had sealed another big business deal.

Perhaps he would take her a gift to show his appreciation.

CHAPTER FOUR

"That's the umpteenth time he has visited the restaurant in the past few weeks," Martha remarked, as she helped Rose prepare another gourmet Amish meal. "And those flowers he got you the other day were beautiful!"

"*Mamm*," Rose said, "the flowers were to show his appreciation of the food which charmed his guests and resulted in another great business deal."

"So he says," Martha whispered, so that only Rose could hear.

"Please, *Mamm*," Rose protested. "We can't talk like this, and especially when our little one is around."

"I won't say anything in front of Luke, or your *daed* and the rest of the family," Martha promised, "if you would tell me what's going on."

Rose stopped lining pie dishes and straightened up. Looking her mother in the eye, she said, "Nothing's going on, *Mamm*. Jason is a good customer—our best—and he obviously thinks that our food is responsible for how well his business deals are going."

"I've seen you two talking," Martha whispered.

Rose returned to lining the pie dishes. They had certainly talked. Jason was interesting. He told her about his horses, and talked about his passion for breeding them. She talked about her work at the restaurant and the inn. But there was one thing she could never bring herself to talk about: Luke.

"Yes, *Mamm*, we talk. It's only polite to be nice to our best customers," Rose replied. "And all the conversations take place only before or after his guests arrive at the restaurant."

"Has he never suggested that you both maybe have coffee together?" Martha asked.

"If he ever did, I would have to say no to that, *Mamm*," Rose replied vehemently.

"But why, child?" Martha queried.

"Because of Luke, of course," Rose said.

She noticed that her mother had stopped what she was doing and was staring at her.

"Oh, my goodness, my Rosie, you have feelings for this man… and you are scared of how he will react to the fact that you have a child already," Martha observed both sympathetically and intuitively.

"I can't talk about this, *Mamm*," Rose said. "Not now, anyway."

"He will surely know about Luke," Martha said, "if he has made inquiries about you."

"Well, then, maybe he hasn't," Rose replied. "Anyway, I had better get this meal out and then go and attend to washing all the table linen."

Later, Rose carried a bag of table linen to the washtub perched on a table outside and began to work the suds up to the brim of the tub.

She had tipped the bag of linen into the tub and was scrubbing each individual tablecloth and napkin when she heard a footfall behind her.

"Rose?" a familiar voice spoke her name.

"Jason!" Rose exclaimed. "I'm sorry, I didn't check on your table after the meal was served. I had some other work to catch up on." When Jason didn't say anything, Rose continued to keep talking. "I hope the meal was to your liking?" she asked.

"My clients were as thrilled as all the other clients have been," Jason replied. "I just want to say thank you for that. You are such a talented chef, and your food is just so… magical."

Rose stopped scrubbing and turned to look at Jason. "Magical?" she breathed. Nobody had ever described her food in quite that manner.

"Yes," Jason answered. "It's made with such expertise, yet with such a very personal touch. It's almost a reflection of you… your personality."

"Oh," Rose murmured, not quite knowing how to react to such a statement. If Jason said her food was magical and if he also said that it was a reflection of her personality, then was she *magical*?

In a few brisk steps, Jason was by her side. Rose looked up at him in surprise.

"Jason!" she said, "what are you doing?"

He had taken off his coat and hung it on a tree nearby, rolled up his sleeves above his elbow, plunged his hands into the washtub and was scrubbing linen.

"What am I doing? Helping you like you have helped me," Jason answered.

"But you can't," Rose said. "You're a guest, my best customer. And it wouldn't be appropriate."

"This Inn, your restaurant, they're all about the authentic Amish experience, are they not?" Jason queried.

"Yes, of course," Rose said, nodding.

"Well then, would you grudge me this? The authentic Amish experience?"

Rose gave him an uncertain smile and shook her head.

She plunged her hands back into the tub and began to scrub a napkin, when she felt something warm against her hand and drew in her breath. Jason's hand had brushed against hers in the suds, and he had allowed it to linger just long enough for the flutter in her belly to escalate to a rapid thumping of her heart. She looked up at him and instantly met his eyes—dark and mysterious. Yet at that moment, his emotions were no mystery, but deeply apparent.

"They're hazel," Jason murmured.

"What are?" Rose whispered, not daring to move her hand away from the spot where it rested against his.

"Your eyes. From the first moment we met, I've been trying to figure out whether your eyes are hazel or amber…"

"*Mamm*!" a voice cried, and Luke came hurtling joyfully out of the door into the yard where Rose and Jason were standing with their arms immersed in the washtub.

"Luke!" Rose said, her arms springing out of the tub. She hastily dried them on her apron and picked Luke up as he flung himself at her in delight.

"I did a picnic," Luke said, "with *Groosdaadi*."

"You mean you went on a picnic with *Groosdaadi*," Rose murmured against Luke's soft cheek.

"This is Luke," Rose said, turning to Jason, hoping to explain how he came to be hers. But Jason had stepped away from the tub and was staring at her almost in anguish.

"I'm so sorry," he said. "I'm so very sorry. I had no idea. I didn't know you were…"

"I'm not…" Rose began to say, but Jason had started to move away.

"What's you name?" Luke piped up, wriggling out of Rose's arms and running to Jason.

Jason stopped short, halted by the little boy. Even as Rose held her breath, he dropped to his knees and took Luke's hand. "I'm Jason. Hello, Luke."

He got to his feet and went to retrieve his coat from the tree.

"I'm sorry, Rose, I have to get home… to work," he said.

Rose said nothing, her spirits plummeting as she watched Jason walk away, without even staying to get an explanation.

***

As Jason drove away, he felt a strange pricking behind his eyes. It was grief and disappointment trying to find expression. He drew the back of his hand over his eyes and kept driving, almost blindly. His vision was hazy, and the only thing on his mind were Luke's eyes, dark-brown and innocent.

Why hadn't Rose told him that she was married and had a baby, Jason lamented. Yet whatever had been building up between them was unmistakable. What was this situation that she was in, and why had nobody thought to mention it to him?

"You're home early," Lydia Lehman observed when her son got home. She eyed him keenly. "Did your business meeting not go well?"

"It went just fine, *Mamm*," Jason replied. "In fact, it went as well as all the others did, thanks to the delightful meal we had during the meeting."

"At Honeycrest Inn?" Lydia queried, smiling indulgently at her son. "Do you honestly think that all your deals go through well because of the food at the restaurant?"

"I do indeed," Jason replied. "Everybody knows that good food and relaxing ambiance are key to doing business."

"Ah, my son the entrepreneur. I am so proud of you," Lydia declared. "But do you know, there is some buzz in the village about you?"

"There is?" Jason asked, sitting down at the kitchen table and pouring himself a glass of water.

"Yes," Lydia said. "People are asking me questions. About whether my son is courting the young girl at Honeycrest."

Jason almost choked on a sip of water.

"How could I be courting her, *Mamm*?" he queried, standing up and staring at his mother, his misery apparent.

"Why not?" Lydia asked. "By all accounts she's a lovely girl and has never been courted before."

"Perhaps you don't know that she has a son, then," Jason declared.

The light of understanding dawned in Lydia's eyes. "Oh, my dear son," she whispered. "You didn't know…"

"No, I didn't know," Jason replied. "And why didn't anyone see fit to tell me?"

"You have obviously developed feelings for Rose Stoltzfus, and you have only just found out about Luke. But son, don't you know the whole story?" Lydia asked.

Jason shook his head. "What is there to know?" he asked.

"This is my fault. It slipped my mind," Lydia said. "The thing is, Jason, Luke is not Rose's own son. He's her late sister's child."

"Oh?" Jason said dully. "He called her *Mamm*."

"Yes, Luke was not even one year old when his parents, Grace and Reuben, were in an accident that took their lives. The Stoltzfus family took over caring for Luke after that, but the little boy literally adopted Rose as his mother, and it made sense that she played that role rather than Rose's parents."

"Why did you never think to share these details with me? Why did Rose herself never tell me?" Jason lamented.

"I have to admit that I never really knew the Stoltzfus family. I never found out about Rose's relationship to Luke until a couple of weeks ago when I made inquiries, because I thought you may be interested in pursuing something long-term with Rose."

"And yet you never told me?" Jason cried.

"To be honest, son, I thought you knew," Lydia said, "and I was waiting for you to tell me. I wondered how you would accept this news, but you seemed quite happy, so I assumed that you must know about Luke, little realizing that you didn't."

"Well, this will change everything, won't it?" Jason murmured.

"I can't see why it has to," Lydia replied. "Rose has done something very noble, and continues to do so. She has done nothing wrong and remains a virtuous young woman who is very eligible."

"I can't discuss this any further, *Mamm*, I'm sorry," Jason said, leaving the room.

***

At the Stoltzfus home, Rose was quietly setting the evening meal on the table and trying to swallow the lump in her throat.

"What's wrong, child?" Martha asked.

"Nothing, *Mamm*," Rose replied.

"Where's Jason?" Luke lisped in his tiny voice.

Rose flushed, and Martha gave her daughter an enquiring look.

"Luke met Jason today," Rose explained tonelessly. "I was outside washing the table linen when Jason came to thank me for the meal… and Luke suddenly appeared… and then Jason…"

"And then Jason?" Martha queried, searching Rose's face for answers.

"I think he got the wrong idea, *Mamm*," Rose said, "and he just rushed away."

"I can go over and explain, if you want me to," Martha said. "You both seemed to be getting closer, and it must hurt."

"It's excruciating," Rose wanted to say, but the words wouldn't get past the lump in her throat, so she merely nodded. "But please don't go over and explain, *Mamm*," she said. "I felt quite humiliated at Jason's reaction, and I never want to go through that again."

"Perhaps he just needed to let this new discovery sink in," Martha said, "and perhaps he needs to know why you never told him about this before—especially when you both were getting to be such good friends."

"I was scared," Rose replied, "and now I see that it was with good reason."

CHAPTER FIVE

"Jason Lehman is here," Martha whispered to Rose. Rose, who was stirring a pot of stew, turned briefly towards her mother and shrugged.

"If someone would take his order, I'll get the food ready," she said, beckoning to one of the waiting staff.

"Mister Lehman wishes to speak to you, Rose," the waitress said, returning quickly to the kitchen.

Rose and Martha exchanged looks, and then Rose shrugged again, smoothed her apron down and went outside to meet Jason.

"Rose," Jason said, his dark, brooding eyes searching hers. "I came to apologize for my behavior the other day."

Rose said nothing, but merely nodded.

"I didn't know about… anything," he continued.

Rose nodded wordlessly again.

"I would like to talk to you away from here," Jason said. "May I?"

"What do you wish to talk about?" Rose asked.

"Everything," Jason said. "Please."

"I will need to bring Luke with me," Rose said. "Because it would not be appropriate for us to go anywhere alone. And it can only be for a short while."

"Of course," Jason replied. "I completely understand."

"He wants to talk," Rose said, returning to the kitchen and untying her apron.

"Go," Martha urged. "I'll take care of things here."

"But *Mamm*, there are guests at the Inn to take care of," Rose said.

"And we have people to handle all that," Martha reassured her. "You go and talk with Jason. I'll take care of the kitchen and Luke."

"No, I'm taking Luke with me," Rose said. "Where is he?"

"With your *daed*. Out in the kitchen garden."

"I'll fetch him. And I'll be back soon, *Mamm*," Rose said.

***

Rose was silent, sitting in the buggy next to Jason. He had taken a quieter route, away from curious eyes, Luke was leaning out the window, his hair tossed by the breeze.

"Where are we headed?" Rose asked finally.

"We'll stop in a minute," Jason replied with a grin.

When the buggy halted, Luke sprang out. Rose stepped off and looked around at the countryside wreathed in shades of spring. It was a pretty spot that Jason had chosen.

"It's safe enough for Luke to play," Jason said, leaning into the buggy and taking out a ball.

Luke's eyes lit up as Jason invited him to catch and throw the ball, and for a while, the two enjoyed this game. Then Luke's attention wandered, and he began to inspect a row of ladybugs meandering through the grass. All the while, Ruth watched them quietly, feeling a strange mix of emotions.

Rose looked apprehensively at Jason.

"Jason, I'm sorry I didn't tell you about Luke before," she said. "I hoped you'd hear from someone else and then ask me, and that would somehow make it easier."

Jason led Rose to a rock and sat down next to her. "Look," he said, "I have to admit I was caught off guard and didn't react very well. I thought Luke was your biological son, and there were all these questions that rose up to torment me. Until I got home, and thankfully my mother told me the truth. She had only just heard, and she thought I might know."

"I see," Rose said.

"I am deeply sorry for your loss," Jason continued. "Losing your sister and brother-in-law so tragically must have hurt terribly. And it must have been very difficult for Luke."

"It was a hard time for us all," Rose said. "But since my sister Grace had once asked me to be there for Luke, and any other children she might have, I had to fulfill my promise to her." Her eyes rested on Luke, playing in the grass, and she smiled. "It wasn't a hard promise to fulfill. I let Luke think of me as his *mamm*, and I tried to be one to him."

"I admire you, Rose," Jason said. "You are a truly good person."

"I'm just doing what I know to be the right thing under the circumstances," Rose replied. "But I shouldn't have kept this from you, and for that I am sorry."

"I suppose I reacted the way I did because I had begun to think of us as friends," Jason explained.

Rose looked down at the hem of her gown, contrite.

"I hope we can still be friends," she said quietly.

"Yes," Jason said. "That's why I wanted to speak to you out here alone."

Rose kept her eyes on the hem of her gown. When Jason didn't say anything further, she raised her eyes to look at him.

"I'm glad we can be friends," she said, finally, and it seemed like everything had fallen flat. She had hoped he would say something more. She had so hoped he would ask her the question that every girl dreams of being asked one day. But maybe friends was all they would be.

She stood up. "I had better get back," she said. "I left my *mamm* handling rush hour and that isn't fair."

"Of course," Jason replied, his voice oddly soft. "I'll take you and Luke back to the Inn."

"What happened?" Martha asked eagerly.

"Nothing really," Rose replied. "Jason played ball with Luke and then apologized to me… and I to him. He said he had asked to speak to me to tell me we can remain friends."

"Oh," Martha murmured. "Well, child, it will take a very unique and special kind of man to agree to be a father to a child that isn't his own. You are unique, Rose, and you deserve somebody equally so."

Later, as Rose was leaving the restaurant to walk across to their home, Martha called after her. "Rose!" she said, "don't forget we need picnic hampers tomorrow! Your *daed* is taking another party of guests out for the day."

"I'll get here earlier, in that case," Rose said. "Don't worry, *Mamm*!"

She woke early the next morning and finished her chores at home—feeding the chickens, picking up the eggs, and milking the cows. Then she washed and dressed, and made her way over to the Inn. In the comfort of her kitchen, she lit the lamps, made herself a cup of hot chocolate, and got to work baking fresh loaves for the picnic sandwiches. Then she cut a leg of roast ham into slices and baked a fresh batch of buttermilk biscuits.

"Hello, Susanna," she greeted her kitchen staff as they came in. "Hello, Sarah!"

As the girls gathered around to help, the picnic feast came together quickly. Rose ran back to the house to wake Luke. She washed and dressed him and gave him his breakfast before hurrying back to the restaurant for the breakfast service.

"I'll bring Luke with me when I come in," Martha said, seeing Rose off at the door.

"Thanks, *Mamm*," Rose said. On an impulse, she turned around and gave her mother a hug. "I'm so glad we have each other," she said.

"He's here," Sarah whispered, as Rose let herself into the kitchen through the rear entrance to the restaurant.

"Who's here?" Rose asked, wrinkling her nose.

"Jason Lehman," Susannah answered, as if she were announcing the visit of royalty.

"But he never comes in for breakfast," Rose remarked, glad they had Scrapple on the menu along with bacon, homemade cheese and preserves.

She announced this to Jason when she went out to greet him a few minutes later.

"Thank you, Rose," Jason said.

"How many guests will be joining you?" Rose asked.

"One young lady… I am hoping," Jason replied.

Rose felt her spirits plummet at Jason's words. Had he actually asked a young lady to join him for breakfast at her restaurant? Luke had certainly made an impression on him, she thought.

"I'll get the food organized, in that case," Rose said, preparing to return to the kitchen.

"Rose," Jason said, halting her. "Would you join me for breakfast, please?"

Rose turned around. "Actually, I have to finish packing picnic hampers and getting ready for lunch service," she said, keeping her voice steady.

"Just a short while in that case?" Jason said, his eyes pleading.

"Alright then," Rose said briskly. "I'll be back after I instruct my kitchen staff."

After taking a few deep breaths in the kitchen to gather herself, Rose returned to the table where Jason sat.

"How have you been?" Jason asked, when Rose had seated herself.

"Very well… and busy," Rose replied.

"And how is Luke?" Jason queried.

"He's well too, and will be here soon," Rose answered.

"That's good. I would love to spend some time with him, if I may," Jason declared.

Rose looked at him questioningly.

"Rose," Jason said, "I would like to get to know you and Luke better."

Rose caught her breath and held it. She was afraid to exhale, lest the moment slip away from her forever.

"What are you saying, Jason?" she asked.

"Rose!" Susannah said, hurrying over to their table. "I'm so sorry to interrupt, but only three buggies have come for the picnickers and we are short of one."

Rose got up from the table. "Where's my *daed*?" she asked.

"There are more guests this time," Susannah replied, "so Mister Stoltzfus is going to be driving his buggy and we still need another. Would you be able to help?"

"I'll have to ask *Mamm* to manage the kitchen today," Rose said, brisk and businesslike, "while I drive my buggy with as many guests as it can take."

Jason was listening to this interchange, and now stood up.

"Rose, may I help, please? I have the whole day free, and I would love to go on one of these picnics I've been hearing so much about. I can take my buggy, so you can manage things here."

Rose looked at him, wondering how to respond.

"Please let me do this," Jason said.

Rose nodded. "Thank you, Jason," she said. The left the restaurant and headed to the Inn together. It was just across the yard.

"Rose, my dear," Martha said, hurrying out the Inn's front door.

"*Mamm*," Rose said, "meet Jason Lehman."

As Jason and her mother exchanged pleasantries, Rose slipped back into the kitchen. Moments later, however, Martha breezed in.

"Rose, that charming young gentleman has requested me to persuade you to go along for this picnic, with Luke, and I think it would do you a world of good to get away for a few hours and enjoy the spring air. I'll take care of the kitchen."

Rose began to open her mouth to protest, when she was aware that they were not alone in the kitchen.

"Please, Rose," Jason said from the doorway.

"Please, *Mamm*," Luke said, peeking out from behind Jason.

"When did Luke get here?" Rose asked Martha.

"He came in with me, of course," Martha said. "Then he went out to play and…"

"…and I found him there and brought him here to persuade you," Jason said.

"This is embarrassing," Rose murmured.

"Please go, Rose," Martha urged.

As they set off in Jason's buggy, with Rose and Luke seated by Jason and three of the Inn guests with them, Rose found herself with nothing much to say to Jason. So she turned to the guests and began to give them a guided tour of the sections of the village which they were passing through. When she couldn't remember some of the details, Jason stepped in and continued the guided tour, so that the narrative went back and forth between them. It was a pleasant way to pass the time during the long buggy ride, and they soon reached their destination—a lake hemmed in by grassy banks, studded with trees and undergrowth.

"This is perfect, isn't it?" Rose said to the guests.

"What is this place called?" they asked.

"This spot is called Green Verge, and we always choose it because it isn't crowded," Rose replied.

"It's perfect," Jason said. "In fact, it would be great to go horseback riding here. Perhaps I can arrange that for your next batch of guests."

"You're very kind," Rose said. She was being reserved, afraid to be vulnerable. She was not sure about her feelings for Jason, yet.

"Jesh," Luke said, tapping Jason on the arm, "I want to go on the horsie."

"Luke, it's Ja-y-son," Rose said.

"Jesh," Luke declared firmly.

"Sure, Luke, I can take you on the horsie," Jason smiled.

"Hello, Rosie!" John Stoltzfus greeted his daughter as he drew up in his buggy.

"Hello, *Daed*!" Rose returned his greeting.

"And this must be Jason Lehman," John said, climbing down from his buggy and helping the guests down.

"Glad to meet you, sir," Jason said.

"*Groosdaadi*, Jesh taking me on the horsie," Luke announced.

"Well, you go off then, young man," John said, giving his grandson a hug and nodding to Jason.

"I'll lay out the picnic hampers on the rugs we've brought along, and let people help themselves when they're ready," Rose said.

"Could we go and explore our surroundings before we eat?" someone asked.

"Alright, but don't wander too far," John cautioned. "It's easy to get lost here." He watched the parties setting off and suddenly called out, "Wait! I'll come with you!"

Rose watched Jason unhitch the horse from his buggy and saddle it.

"Where did you get the saddle from?" Rose asked.

"I always carry one in my buggy, just in case I lose a wheel and have to ride instead," Jason said. He lifted Luke up into the saddle and climbed on behind him.

"Don't worry," he said to Rose, who was looking anxiously up at them, "we won't go far, and we will be back soon."

After Jason had trotted off with Luke and the picnickers had scattered, some with her father and the others in twos and threes, Rose busied herself spreading rugs on the banks and laying out the picnic hampers. It was a beautiful day and the fresh spring air was invigorating. Rose hadn't been out to a picnic in a very long while, and she felt herself relax and enjoy the peace.

She sat on a rock and stared out over the lake, all her cares cast aside by the tranquil blue waters, the ripples reflecting shafts of light that they caught from the sun as it drifted in and out from the clouds above. And suddenly she was caught in a daydream—a luxury that she seldom allowed herself. In this pleasant fantasy, Jason was walking towards her with a smile, secrets unveiled in his mysterious dark eyes as they were when her hands had brushed against his in the suds that blissful day that now seemed so long ago.

"Rose?" he said, his voice deep and resonant.

"Yes?" Rose whispered into the silence, her eyes closed as she leaned back against the rock and sank deeper into the fantasy.

"Would you say yes, if I asked to court you?"

"Yes, yes, I will," Rose whispered.

"*Mamm*?" Luke's voice broke through her fantasy, and Rose sprang up, embarrassed at seeing Jason watching her curiously.

"Oh! How long have you been standing there?" she asked Jason.

"You kept saying *yes*," Jason said with a smile, "quite dreamily, I might add."

"I must have drifted off to sleep and was dreaming," Rose said briskly, jumping to her feet and smoothing her gown down. "I woke up far earlier this morning to get the food ready for the picnic…"

"It's alright to be relaxed outdoors, Rose," Jason said with a chuckle.

"How was your ride, Luke?" Rose asked her nephew, ready to take Jason's attention off of her for a bit.

"I'm going again!" Luke replied.

"Are you going off again now?" Rose asked Jason.

"In a little while," Jason answered. "But I came back to ask if you'd like to ride too."

"Me?" Rose queried. "Oh no. Perhaps another time." She squinted into the distance as she stood, facing away from the lake. "What's going on there?" she asked.

"It seems like everybody's coming back," Jason replied.

"They seem to be in some distress," Rose remarked, "judging from the speed at which they are running. "I hope they aren't being pursued by some wild beast!"

"No wild beasts here that I know of," Jason said. "But if you like, I can go and find out what's happening."

Rose looked at the picnic hampers laid out and shrugged. "I think I'll come along too, and hopefully the hampers will still be here when we get back," she said.

"Help!" Rose heard someone cry. "We need help!"

Rose took Luke's hand and began to run towards the picnickers, who were hurrying their way in obvious distress.

"We need a horse or two!" someone cried.

"What's wrong?" Rose asked, looking back to see if any of the buggy drivers were nearby.

"I'll get my horse," Jason said, running back to where he had tethered his horse by a tree.

"It's my *daed*!" Rose cried, when Jason galloped back. "He's in trouble!"

"It was a pit. It covered over with undergrowth, and nobody realized there was a hole there until John stepped onto the undergrowth and fell into the pit," one of the guests explained breathlessly. "He may have twisted an ankle when he fell in. We need help quick!"

"Oh no!" Rose said, visibly alarmed.

"Rose, stay here with Luke," Jason said. "I'll go and get your *daed*, don't worry.

"No, I need to come with you, Jason, please," Rose said. "I'll bring Luke too. I'll follow your horse on foot."

"That will take too long," Jason replied. "Come on, jump up behind me," he instructed. "But hand me, Luke, first. I'll hold him in front."

Rose climbed onto the horse behind Jason. She realized it wasn't ladylike to ride astride in a gown, but she had no choice, anxious as she was about her father.

Jason had set off at a gallop, and Rose was forced to hold onto him.

"Don't worry, Rose," Jason reassured her as they rode along. "It will be alright. We'll have your *daed* out of that pit soon."

"Maybe we should have brought some rope along," Rose said, worried.

"It's all there in the saddlebag," Jason replied. "I'm just going to speed up a little. "Hold on, Luke. Hold on, Rose!"

Moments later, they were at the site of the mishap. Jason jumped off the horse and swung Luke down. Rose was in the process of trying to climb down when Jason lifted her off the horse. Caught in his strong arms for a moment, Rose felt that same familiar flutter in her tummy, but it was soon replaced by fear for her father.

The moment her feet were on the ground she ran to where a group of the picnickers were calling down the pit to John and telling him that help was on the way.

"*Daed*! We're here!" Rose called down, and was relieved when her father called back.

"Rose! Don't you worry now. I'm fine. I'll be better, of course, once I get out of here."

Rose stood back, clutching Luke and Jason's coat which he had taken off and handed to her. He lowered a rope down to John after tying the other end to a tree. He is so strong, Rose thought, gazing at Jason, his sleeves rolled up to reveal his muscled forearms.

"Stand back!" Jason cried, and everybody moved.

But it was harder than they anticipated to get John out of the pit. He was finding it difficult to climb the rope because of a stabbing pain in his ankle.

Jason beckoned to some of the men. "Hold on to the rope behind me and pull for all you're worth," he instructed.

Rose watched Jason in admiration. He was so masterful, so strong, so in control, she thought to herself.

"Don't worry, Mister Stoltzfus, sir," Jason called out. "We're going to pull you up. Don't move a muscle. Just hold on to the rope."

Rose began to pray silently, and even Luke was quiet and tense.

The men began to pull on the rope as Jason directed them, and suddenly they saw the top of John's head.

"*Daed*!" Rose sobbed in relief as John's shoulders emerged above the rim of the pit and the men darted forward to help Jason lift him out.

The sound of cheering drowned out Rose's sobbing. She fell to her knees by her father, trying to locate the injury.

"Rosie," John reassured his daughter. "It's just a sprain. It will be fine soon. I'm just lucky it's nothing worse."

"We got a buggy to take you back," one of the guests said.

"Thank you so much," Rose said. "You all are wonderful, and so thoughtful."

"Let's go back to the lake and enjoy our picnic," John said. "I can get my ankle tended to after that."

"*Daed*, no, you need to get home and to a doctor," Rose protested, but John was insistent that the day not be spoiled for the picnickers.

"I can fix a makeshift splint to your ankle," Jason said, and set about getting John comfortable and attending to his ankle.

CHAPTER SIX

"I don't know how to thank you," Rose said to Jason. "I'm so glad you were there… and that I was there too."

"Rose," Jason said, "remember before we got caught up with going on the picnic?"

"Yes?" Rose murmured.

"I was going to ask you something," Jason said.

"What were you going to ask me, Jason?" Rose asked.

"I was going to ask you if you would consider letting me court you," Jason said.

"Oh," Rose whispered, her heart beginning to do a little tap dance. It was just like her fantasy.

"But I've changed my mind about that now," Jason declared.

"Oh," Rose said, her heart slowing down and her spirits plummeting. "It's because of Luke, isn't it?"

"You're right," Jason said. "It is because of Luke. It took me just one short horse ride with him to know I could so easily be a *daed* to him."

"What?" Rose said, her eyes flying up to Jason's.

"Oh, Rose," Jason said. "I don't want to ask to court you. Oh no, I don't want to waste any time or any more of my life living without you. I have looked for you all my life and now that I've found you, how could I let you go? Please, my Rose, would you marry me?"

His dark, mysterious, mesmerizing eyes were boring into hers. His hand reached out to gently touch her cheek. A tremor went through her.

"Jason," she said, "are you sure?"

"How couldn't I be?" Jason whispered. "I've known from the moment I saw you looking out of the window before you turned to look at me. I saw your eyes, your lovely hazel eyes. Do you know, Rose, your eyes speak volumes? You never had to speak, and yet I knew everything that you felt. But I also knew, because I felt it, too—overwhelmingly." He tilted her chin up to look deeper into her eyes.

"But just now, I need to hear you say what I see in those beautiful eyes," he whispered.

"Oh Jason, how could it be anything but *yes*?" Rose whispered back.

The End

Please Check out My Other Works

By checking out the link below

http://cleanromancepublishing.com/rbauth

Thank You

Many thanks for taking the time to buy and read through this book.

It means lots to be supported by SPECIAL readers like YOU.

Hope you enjoyed the book; please support my writing by leaving an honest review to assist other readers.

.

With Regards,

Ruth Bawell